Black

Written By

Julie Thorpe

To Helen

Enjoy!

JThorpe

This is a work of fiction.

Names, characters, organisations, places, events and incidences are either products of the author's imagination or used fictitiously.

Copyright 2021 by Julie Thorpe.

All rights reserved.

No part of this book may be reproduced, or stored in a retrieval system, or transmitted in any form or by any means, electronic, mechanical, photocopying, recording, or otherwise without the express written permission of the publisher.

Independently published via Kindle Direct Publishing.

Cover created by Cassie Robbins.

Prologue.

"This sucks."

I sighed as I kicked the tyre in frustration. The date had gone badly and the car breaking down was the last thing I needed. When Tim had asked me out on a date, I'd thought sure why not? He was a nice guy and we got along great. So when I turned up and found him already drunk, unable to form coherent sentences, I was more than a little disappointed. On my way back to the car he had followed me, begging for me to stop and talk with him but I refused until I heard a low moan. Turning around, I saw that he'd fallen over and was now laying sprawled out across the floor with his head lolling to the side. I sighed.

"This sucks."

I pulled my phone out and searched for the number for Johnny, our mutual friend. As soon as it was located, I pressed dial and turned to gaze down on the man who had now passed out. Ugh, what a mess. I heard a click as the phone connected.

"Hello? Marie, is everything alright?" said the voice on the other end.

"Not really. Your buddy is passed out in the carpark, drunk. Any chance you can come and pick him up?" I answered bluntly. I heard a low curse from his end.

"Are you kidding me? He's drunk?"

"Yep. Didn't even get to have our date, he was already like it when I got here."

"He's such an idiot. Yeah, I'll come pick him up. Which carpark is it?" Johnny asked, the irritation evident in his tone.

"The one behind Newman's. That's where we were supposed to meet up. I'll wait till you get here and then I'm gone. Will you be long?" I queried, glancing quickly at the phone screen to check the time. 7:10pm. I rolled my eyes, replacing the phone to my ear. What a rubbish night.

"About twenty minutes? I'll be as quick as I can," came his reply. I could hear some shuffling on his end and wondered briefly what he was doing. I agreed and hung up the phone. I made my way over to my car a couple of feet away and opened it up. I'd sit inside and wait for Johnny to pick up my drunken date. After a few minutes, I shivered as the cold of the evening began to seep inside and under my skin. I put the key in the ignition and turned the car on, hoping to put the heater on to warm me up. *Screech!* The engine died before it even started up.

"What the-" I muttered, leaning forwards to shift my weight as I tried again.

Screech! The exact same sound and the engine died once more. I flopped against the back of my seat in disbelief.

"Is this a joke? What a crap night!"

I let out a frustrated growl and quickly tapped onto the app on my phone to alert the breakdown service that I was stuck. According to that app, they would be here in an hour.

"Great," I grumbled. "At least Johnny will be here soon."

I got back out of the car and walked back over to Tim, grabbing a blanket out of my car boot to cover him up. He might be an ass for turning up drunk and then passing out, but I wasn't about to let him get sick just because I didn't cover him up and keep him warm. I wasn't having that on my conscience. Once that was done, I went back to my car and kicked the tyre, letting my frustration out on it. I leaned back against it, resting my head in my hands as I tried to think of how this night could have possibly gone instead. We could have had a nice meal, drinks and then either gone on to a bar or called it a night. That would've been preferable to this mess.

As I lifted my head, I noticed a person heading over to me across the carpark. I furrowed my brow as I concentrated on them, wondering what was wrong with them. It looked like a man but he was walking strangely. His right leg seemed to be dragging with his steps, not quite leaving the ground and leaving him with a limp. As he got closer, I stared when I could make his face out clearly. The skin was mottled and grey with the skin around his mouth apparently eroded away so there was nothing covering his teeth. I realised his clothes were torn and when I saw the vacant expression in his eyes, I realised the truth of what I was seeing. I moved along the side of my car until I reached the hood of it, putting as much distance between myself and the dead man as I could without alerting him to my rising fear. He was still making his way towards me but slowly, giving me enough time to get away. Or so I thought.

I crept backwards from him, not turning away as he approached. I wanted to keep my eyes on him. Another step backwards and I bumped into something solid. Startled, I spun on my feet to find myself faced with another one of these creatures. A female this time. I took several steps away from her, unable to tear my eyes from the grisly sight that stood before me. The man looked great compared to this person. The hair was long but patchy, bald spots vivid upon the waxy skull that housed dark pockets that had once held eyes. The skin was paper thin and stretched across the skull, as it was on the other parts of her body that I could see. What had once been a dress hung loosely from her body in shreds, barely covering the shrivelled corpse.

I gagged at the sight. How were these people here? I'd heard of the undead but never believed it for one second but how can you dispute something that is staring you in the face? I covered my mouth at the sight of her, hoping I wouldn't be sick. This couldn't be happening! I shot a glance over my shoulder towards the other creature and noticed he'd gone past Tim, ignoring him as he made his way over to me. I frowned. Weren't these things supposed to want to eat anyone? Yet he was after me and had left Tim alone! Talk about irony that my date was safe and sound in his unconscious state. I saw something moving out of the corner of my eye in the darkness. I squinted in that direction as I began to run from both creatures, hoping that what I was seeing would be someone who could help. As the person stepped into the light, I cried out in horror. Another creature. Where the hell were these things coming from? I skidded to a halt, swivelling on my heel to head in another direction only to come to another stop. There were more creatures behind me now that I hadn't seen before. My palms sweating, I searched for a way out of this throng of monsters. Horrified, I realised I was trapped. There were dozens of them now, surrounding me on all sides. How had they moved so quickly? The first two had been so slow!

Hahaha!

I heard laughter carrying across the wind towards me, loud and clear even in the midst of this madness. I quickly scanned the carpark for the origin of the voice, hoping it could be some sort of help. I didn't get a chance to see who it was. The creatures were almost upon me, their bodies blocking my view as I desperately searched for an opening to escape. One of the creatures bit into the back of my neck and I screamed, trying to wrench myself away only for another to grab my arm and take a bite. I beat at them, fighting against my impending doom as much as I could but in the end, it was to no avail. The pain was too much as they leapt upon my body, pulling me to the ground as they took chunks out of me.

The light had long passed from my eyes before they were finished.

Chapter One.

"Hi Anna! Did you hear what happened last night?"

I glanced up at Tina as she sat herself down across from me and began rummaging in her bag for her lunch. I raised an eyebrow at her, shaking my head to indicate no as my mouth was full. She slid her packed sandwiches onto the table between us and got herself settled properly before telling me the news she wanted to share.

"Marie was killed last night!"

I stared at her, my mouth hanging open ready for the food that I'd just been about to eat. I set the food back down on the table and gaped at my colleague.

"Are you serious?" I questioned, unable to comprehend what I'd just heard. She nodded vigorously at me, shoving her sandwich into her mouth for a bite. Without waiting to finish chewing, she answered me.

"Yep. Apparently Johnny found her. She was all torn up so I heard."

"Oh jeez. That's awful! Poor Marie and poor Johnny! He found her? Where was she?" I asked, slightly disgusted by the fact she was still stuffing her face. How could she eat with this news hanging over us? I'd completely lost my appetite at the news but there she was, munching away on that sandwich. She took a second to swallow then replied.

"She was in the Newman's carpark. Johnny went to pick up Tim 'cus he was passed out drunk and Marie was supposed to be there so Johnny went looking and found what was left of her. It's why he didn't come in to fix the fire exit door today, took it pretty hard by all accounts," Tina paused for a second, eyeing up the food in front of me. "Hey, are you going to finish that?"

"It's all yours," I muttered, pushing my food towards her as I picked up my bag to leave.

"Where are you going?"

I looked down at her, unable to hide the utter contempt I had for this woman from my face now.

"I'm going back to work. I don't know how you can eat after telling me such awful news and knowing our friend is dead. I'll see you later," I told her, turning to stride away before she said anything else. If I stayed, I knew I'd do something I'd regret. I made my way down the hallway, heading towards my classroom as I pondered upon what Tina had told me. Marie had died! I knew her through work and we'd become good friends over the years. She'd always been such a lovely person so for her to be killed was just horrific. I felt terrible for Johnny. He'd always been there, playing protector for everyone in the village and helping out when needed. He had such a big heart so for him to have witnessed something so awful, I couldn't imagine how he must be feeling. As I reached the door to my classroom, I decided that I was going to go and see him once I'd finished work to check on him.

Five o'clock rolled around sooner than I realised. School had finished a little while earlier but I'd stayed behind to mark homework as I often did before heading home. I liked my personal time to remain my own, not having to mark papers at home. I packed up my things and headed out to my car, slinging my bag onto the backseat as I slid into the driver seat. Checking the coast was clear, I pulled out of my space and found my way to the road to head to Johnny's. He didn't live too far from the school as he was the local handyman and with all the breakages we ended up with from the children, he would be at the school most days so it made sense that he lived close by.

My palms grew sweaty as I came to a halt outside his house. He would be a mess, I knew he would be. How could he not be after witnessing something so horrible? I wasn't sure how I was going to handle this but he needed to know that his friends were there for him. To know he had a support system to get him through this. I took a deep breath, squared my shoulders and got out of the car. I walked along his front pathway and rapped hard on the fine wooden door in front of me. I waited patiently, shifting slightly from one foot to the other. I was nervous about seeing Johnny. I'd had a crush on him since we were little but I'd never done anything about it. I didn't want to ruin the friendship and I sincerely hoped he'd never picked up on the vibes. I didn't want him to think I was there for selfish reasons, I just wanted to know he was alright.

I heard the key turn in the lock a moment before the door opened, revealing a dishevelled Johnny. He looked awful! His skin was pasty white, the dark circles under his eyes deep. The expression on his face was one of defeat and hopelessness. It pained my heart to see him like this. Johnny was always the life of the party, the big brother of the group. Now, he just seemed so lost. He gave me a wan smile.

"Hey Anna."

"Hi Johnny," I replied with a small smile. "I heard what happened and wanted to come and check on you."

His eyes dulled at my words, his head nodding a couple of times.

"I had a feeling you would. You've got a good heart Anna. I'm not great company at the moment but you're welcome to come in if you want to."

"Thanks," I muttered, following him inside and closing the door behind me. He motioned for me to go with him into the kitchen so I did. Once inside, Johnny made his way over to the kettle.

"What would you like to drink?" he asked, pulling two mugs from the overhead cupboard and flipping the switch for the kettle to boil.

"Coffee is fine. Two sugars, thanks," I told him as I cast my eyes about the kitchen as he set himself to making the drinks. It was pristine. I shouldn't have been surprised as Johnny had always been tidy but I was still surprised all the same. I briefly wondered if he'd eaten anything today.

"How are you holding up?" I questioned him softly, noticing the way his shoulders tensed at my question whilst he poured the water into the mugs. He didn't answer me right away, instead taking the time to finish making the drinks and handed me one. He finally allowed himself to raise his eyes and look at me, sighing as he did so. He scrubbed a hand over his face.

"Not great, but you can probably see that for yourself," he muttered, gesturing for me to sit at the table with him. I pulled a chair out and sat down, holding my mug between my hands for warmth. I stayed quiet, allowing him to speak in his own time. I sensed I shouldn't push him on this. He could talk to me if he wanted to but on his own terms. He took a sip of his coffee, peering at me over the top of his mug. He smiled wryly at me.

"Thanks for coming to see me. Other than the police, you're actually the first person I've seen today," he told me. I gasped at that. How could nobody have checked in on him? I took in his appearance once more. His usually tidy hair was sticking up in various directions from his hands running through it most likely, the usual chocolate colour seeming dull today. Stubble had appeared on his chin and his blue eyes were dull and lifeless. Whatever he had seen had truly horrified him. He was wearing a grey t-shirt and a pair of jeans, both faded and stained with paint. He must have just thrown on the nearest thing to him when he woke up.

"I'm a bit concerned no one else has been to see you. I came as soon as I finished work. Do you want to talk about it?" I asked him gently, not wanting to make him feel as though he had to discuss it. I saw the hesitation on his face but then the tension disappeared from his posture as he took a deep breath.

"I don't but I feel like I need to, you know? Marie had gone to Newman's to meet Tim for a date but the idiot got drunk and passed out. So Marie called me up asking if I could pick Tim up and I agreed. She said she'd wait until I got there but when I arrived, she wasn't there. Her car was though and I found it strange, so I had a look about the car to see if anything seemed off. Other than Tim lying on the ground, it all seemed normal until I reached the other side of the car." He took in a shuddering breath. "What I saw...there's no words to truly describe it. I recognised it was Marie because of her hair but that was it. She was torn apart! I called the police immediately and when they arrived, they kept insisting that an animal had done it but Anna," he paused and stared right at me, "I don't know of any animal that could do that kind of damage to a person."

I gaped at him, horrified by the tale he was telling me. The pleading expression on his face to believe him shook me. Had it truly been that bad? What could this poor man have seen to make him say that? I reached out and touched his hand tentatively, wrapping my fingers around his and squeezing reassuringly.

"What do you think it was if you don't think it was an animal? What else did the police say?" I asked him, keeping my voice low and calm. My heart pounded in my chest, a contradiction to my outer self I was presenting to him. He shook his head in defeat.

"I don't know. I really don't know but it wasn't an animal. I would bet my life that it wasn't but it couldn't have been human either. And do you know what else was weird about last night?"

I shook my head, waiting patiently for him to continue. His lips had pursed as his face scrunched into a confused expression.

"I saw Cara as I headed into the carpark last night. I saw her walking out of there and she was laughing! There's no way that she couldn't have seen something but when I told the police that she was there and they questioned her, she denied having been there and they believed her! No more questions asked!" he exclaimed, his grip on his mug visibly tightening. I frowned at that. It did seem a bit odd that she'd denied being there if he saw her.

"Yeah, that's weird. Are you sure she would've seen something though? She could've just been using the back entrance out of Newman's and might not have seen anything?" I asked but he was already shaking his head.

"There's no way. When I first saw her, she was walking away from the car. From Marie's car! She definitely saw *something* and she was laughing! I think she might have been involved, I just don't know how."

I let go of his hand, placing it back around the mug as I studied him. If what he was saying was true then it certainly implicated Cara but he did say he didn't know what could have done such a horrible thing to

Marie. How could Cara have pulled her apart? She was such a slight figure of a woman that a strong wind could blow her over. I shook my head at him, unwilling to believe that woman could have anything to do with this tragic event.

"How could she have been involved? You said yourself that no human could have done what you saw. Cara's lovely, she wouldn't hurt a fly!"

Johnny stared at me as if I'd just slapped him in the face.

"You don't believe me?"

I sighed, not knowing how to say what I wanted without offending him further.

"I believe that you saw something absolutely awful last night and I believe that you saw Cara. I don't know why she would lie about being there but I do believe you when you say you saw her. I just don't know if she could have been involved." At the look of pure disbelief on his face, I hastened on with my words. "It's not that I don't believe you Johnny, it's just that she's a nice girl and she's got no strength to her. I can't imagine her hurting anyone but I think we need to find out what she was doing there. Maybe that can explain more about her if nothing else?"

Johnny pulled his lip up in a sneer, the disappointment and annoyance plain to see upon his face. He pushed his chair away from the table and stood up, plucking his mug from the surface and moving over to the kitchen sink to rinse it out.

"You should go."

I gawked at him, feeling awkward all of a sudden. Damn, I'd really put my foot in it with him hadn't I? I raised myself up to my feet, picked up my mug and took it over to him at the sink. Placing it by his side on the counter, I glanced at his face and immediately wished I hadn't. The anger on his face was unlike anything I'd ever seen on him before.

"I'm sorry," I muttered. I turned and got out of there as quickly as I could.

Chapter Two.

I sat in my car, wondering if I was doing the right thing.

I knew I'd hurt Johnny by not believing in him but I still didn't understand how he thought sweet Cara could be involved in the death of our friend. Cara had moved here a few months back, all alone and told us she was getting over some family drama. Since then, she had become a pillar of our community, helping with the various charity days that were set up and was generally kind to everyone she came across. To imagine her capable of being an accomplice to murder just didn't seem possible. No, it wasn't possible at all. Except that look in Johnny's eyes was haunting me. He said he saw her at Newman's and I really did believe that part of the story so it didn't sit right with me that she had lied to the police about being there. So I was sat in my car outside her house, working up the courage to go and ask her what had happened. If I could just get the information on why she was there and keeping it secret, I could go back to Johnny with it and let him see that I really did believe him that she was there. I got out of the car and made my way up the short path to her house. Cara owned a pretty little cottage with white bricks and a thatched roof. Ivy wound up the sides of the walls with purple wisteria flowers flowing down from the roof. In the twilight, these plants made the house appear darker, more ominous than I'd recalled it ever being before. I stopped walking for a moment, taking in the sight of the house properly. Perhaps it was what Johnny had said about Cara but I had a strange sense of foreboding as I gazed upon the little cottage. I saw the lights were on inside and a shadow moved about along the wall I could see through the window. I crossed the remaining few feet to the front door and rapped sharply on the glass panels that decorated the top half of the door. I saw when she made her way towards me, taking a step backwards instinctively.

Cara smiled brightly at me as she swung the door inwards to reveal the small hallway behind her.

"Hi Anna! What can I do for you?" she asked.

I smiled at her, hoping she wouldn't notice that I was nervous.

"I wondered if I could possibly have a quick word with you if that's alright?"

"Of course. Come on in," she said, holding the door wider for me to enter the cottage. I passed her and waited as she closed the door, before following her into her living room. I hadn't been inside the cottage before and it wasn't how I'd expected it to be. The interior had warm colours as I'd thought it would but there was an atmosphere in the air that made my earlier feeling of foreboding grow. I couldn't place what was making me feel that way, the furniture and the personal objects around the living room all seemed to fit with the caring and warm nature of the woman in front of me, but there seemed a sense of danger too. I took it all in as Cara sat down upon the cream sofa, gesturing towards me to do the same. I perched on the edge of my seat, feeling uneasy.

"So what did you want to have a word with me about?" Cara questioned, her eyes gazing at me expectantly. I laced my fingers together and rested them in my lap to stop myself from fidgeting.

"It's a bit of a delicate subject if I'm honest. You heard about Marie last night didn't you?" I began, knowing full well that she had but I wanted to see if she'd lie to me. She nodded her head, a sad expression appearing on her face.

"Yes. It's just awful news isn't it?"

"Yes it is," I replied, relieved that she'd begun with honesty. "Well, Johnny found her body and he says that he saw you walking away from her car just as he got there, but apparently you told the police that you weren't there?"

A frown marred her features and her eyes narrowed slightly at me.

"Yes, that's right. I did tell the police that."

"Why?"

"Why what?" she asked me, her tone taking on a slight edge. I paused as I observed her, realising that Johnny had been right about her being there. If she was innocent, she wouldn't have suddenly become cagey about it. I took another steadying breath.

"Why did you tell them that? You were there."

"No I wasn't. What are you insinuating?" she asked me sharply, her whole demeanour changing now as her eyes remained fixed on mine. Uncomfortable, I decided to pretend I'd seen her myself and see what she said to that. If she still denied it, then I wasn't sure what I could do but I had no doubt in my mind now that she was lying. Cara wasn't as innocent as she made herself out to be and I could see it as plain as day.

"I don't understand why you're lying to me. I saw you too, it wasn't just Johnny who saw you."

I saw the nice persona slip from her in an instant, a sneer curling her top lip upwards.

"So prove it. No one will believe you, the police certainly won't. They've already dismissed me as having been there," she informed me bluntly. I gaped at her in shock. Had she really just said that?

"You admit it then?" I asked. She shrugged.

"Why deny it? You saw me so you know I was there."

"Why are you lying to the police though? Did you have something to do with Marie's death?" I knew I was playing with fire by asking the question but I needed to know if Johnny's suspicions had been right after all.

"No of course I didn't! What do you take me for?" she snapped, crossing her arms in front of her chest defensively. I held my hands up in mock surrender.

"I'm sorry for asking but it just seems odd that you won't tell the police you were there. Did you see something? Were you threatened? Help me to understand so I can tell Johnny. Please," I pleaded with her. I watched as she slowly unfurled her arms, her posture relaxing a little bit as her face smoothed out and took on the usual pleasant expression that I had become accustomed to seeing on her face over the years. The horrible personality she had begun to show disappeared completely as the false nicer version came back into play.

"I didn't see anything, I promise," she uttered, smiling at me now. "I was there meeting up with a member of the village committee because he's arranging a secret surprise for his wife. I was sworn to secrecy so when the police asked me about Marie's death, I denied being there because I didn't want my friend's wife to find out about her surprise ahead of time. That's all. I didn't see anything so I didn't see the harm in it. You won't tell anyone about this though, will you?" She leaned forwards and placed her hand on my arm, biting her lip nervously.

I gaped at the complete turn around from her snapping at me one minute to being nice again the next. It didn't make sense. I could tell from the way she was acting that she was hiding more than just a secret surprise for some committee member's wife but I didn't push it. I needed to get out of there before she realised I didn't believe her.

"No, no of course I won't. Don't want to ruin any surprises," I replied, a small smile on my face. "Thankyou for answering my questions and I apologise for intruding on your time. I'll head off now."

I rose from my seat, telling her I'd see myself out and headed out of the house to my car. I closed the door behind me as I slipped into the driver seat and let out a shaky breath. Glancing back towards the cottage, I saw Cara stood at the window. I gave her a brief wave and started the car up. Cara remained where she was, watching me as I drove away from her and her creepy cottage.

I had to get back to Johnny. He needed to know that I believed him now. Cara had been involved with Marie's death, of that there was no doubt.

Chapter Three.

Banging on Johnny's door, I grew impatient when he didn't answer it.

I banged on the wood once more, louder this time and for longer.

"Alright alright! I'm coming!" came his deep voice. As soon as he opened the door, I pushed my way past him and made my way towards his kitchen. I heard him grumbling as he shut the door behind me and followed to where I was standing. I faced him, noting that he hadn't changed from when I'd seen him earlier except that he was now frowning at me and his brows were furrowed together.

"What's going on? Why'd you barge in like that?" he demanded. I took a deep breath.

"You were right. Cara was involved in Marie's death somehow. I don't know how but she was."

There, I'd said it. His eyes widened as his jaw went slack. After a second or two, he gave his head a brief shake before taking a step towards me, his whole body suddenly tense.

"What's happened? You didn't believe it before but you do now so I'm guessing something's happened?" he queried, concern showing on his face.

I nodded my head, my thoughts running rampant through my mind. How was she involved? Perhaps she owned some crazy animal that had done it? I sighed as I took a seat at the table in the same place I'd been a mere few hours earlier as Johnny took the one opposite me. He waited, his eyebrow perched up in silent question.

"I went to see her," I began. I saw Johnny's eyes bulge at this news but he remained silent so I could continue. "I didn't think she was involved in the death as you know, but I was certain that you had seen her so it was bugging me why she lied to the police about it. So, I decided to go see her and ask her."

"You actually asked her? Outright to her face?" Johnny asked, incredulity in his tone.

"Yeah. I know, bad idea but I needed to know. At first she denied it but the way she was being all defensive, I could tell she was lying. So I made up a little lie of my own and asked her to tell the truth because I'd seen her too."

I heard a sharp intake of breath from Johnny. I glanced at his face and saw the alarm showed there. I smiled at him in reassurance.

"It's alright. It worked because then she completely stopped being fake and told me I could never prove it. She wasn't going to deny being there after I said I'd seen her but she wasn't going to tell the police either." I paused as I shifted my weight in the chair a bit, trying to steel myself for what I was about to tell him. "It was really weird. When I asked her about Marie, she told me she hadn't been involved. Snapped at me in fact. Then she changed all of a sudden back into the nice Cara that we all know and told me the reason she was at

Newman's was that she was meeting a committee member there who was arranging a surprise for his wife. Apparently it's all meant to be a secret so she told the police she hadn't been there to prevent the surprise from being ruined."

Johnny stared at me in utter disbelief. He ran a calloused hand through his dark hair, keeping his blue eyes trained on me.

"You don't believe her do you?" he muttered. It wasn't really a question but more of a statement. I shook my head in answer anyway.

"Nope. Not a bit. I'm fairly sure she thinks I do but after seeing her changing personalities in such a short space of time, I don't believe her story at all. She was far too defensive for an innocent person to behave. I just don't know why or how she was involved."

Johnny gave me a relieved little smile.

"Thankyou," he said as he reached out and took my hand in his. "Thankyou for believing me and checking her story out even when you weren't sure. Thing is, I don't know what to do now."

I shrugged, my eyes fixed on our intertwined hands. His palms felt both rough and smooth at the same time, warm and safe. I cleared my throat when I realised I hadn't answered him and raised my eyes back to his. I felt my cheeks begin to flame when I saw the slight smile tugging at the corner of his lips. Dammit! He'd noticed.

"Yeah, I'm not sure what we do now either to be honest but we can't let her get away with it. Should we just, I don't know, watch her for a few days? It's only Thursday so I've got work tomorrow but I can help from tomorrow night and over the weekend?" I asked him, trying to come up with some sort of plan.

"Yeah, that sounds like a plan. I can watch her tomorrow because I'm not going back to work this week. I need to make sure our friends are safe. How's about you meet me here at six tomorrow night and we'll go from there?" Johnny asked.

I agreed. What else could I do? If Cara really had helped with killing Marie, what was to stop her from doing it again to someone else?

***

Six o'clock on Friday night rolled around quicker than I expected.

The day had been a busy one, my students keeping me on my toes all day. They were all excited about the upcoming charity party we were having in a few weeks and they all wanted to be involved. As I was organising the food, a lot of the children had been coming to me with suggestions for food ideas or to offer me their help in the run up to the party. I was extremely pleased with my students for offering their help as I knew a lot of children might think it uncool to help their teacher, but my bunch of students were extremely helpful and conscientious of those around them. The charity party had even been their idea so I couldn't be any prouder of them than I already was.

As soon as I finished work, I raced home and got changed into more comfortable clothing before making my way back to Johnny's. A pair of black leggings and a pale pink top would be fine for wherever we had to go. I arrived just before six o'clock so I took a few minutes to allow myself to relax, ensuring I was calm and collected before I met him. My stomach was doing somersaults at the prospect of spending the weekend with him, albeit on Cara watch but still, I was secretly pleased by the turn of events. Then my mind slipped back to thinking about Marie and I mentally chastised myself for being so selfish. Poor Marie had lost her life and there was me getting all giddy over a weekend with my crush. Come on Anna, get a grip!

I tutted at myself as I got out of the car, slamming the silver door behind me in frustration. Johnny just needed a friend, not some idiot fawning over his every move. I rapped sharply on his door, surprised when he pulled it open almost instantaneously.

He peered outside, saw me and gave me a wide grin. Stepping outside, he turned and locked the door as I observed him. This was the Johnny I was used to. He was wearing jeans and a smart top with trainers and his hair had been combed. When I saw his face, it still seemed haunted but there was a sense of determination about him too. He wrapped his arms around me in a hug and whispered into my ear.

"I've followed her all day. She's supposed to be meeting someone for a drink in half an hour at the café."

I took the hint from him that he was trying to keep things quiet so as not to arouse suspiscion so I pulled back, gave him a wide smile and tugged on his hand.

"Come on Johnny, let's go for that drink. We haven't got all night you know."

I saw the flash of admiration on his face as I turned around, pulling him along behind me. Those somersaults in my stomach kept on flipping over. We got into the car and I pulled away from the kerb into the road and drove us to the café.

"So what's happened today? Did you see anything incriminating?" I asked him as we drove. I could feel his eyes on me as I stayed focused on the steering wheel, beginning to feel self conscious as we made our way to the café.

"Nothing out of the ordinary happened," he answered. "She was in her house for a while, went to work this afternoon then I overheard her chatting to someone on the phone arranging to meet so that's what we're doing now. Perhaps it'll be someone who can give us some clues."

I grunted my agreement, distracted by the driving until I came to a stop outside the café. I parked up on the other side of the road and peered out through my window to see if Cara was already there.

"Can you see her?" Johnny queried. I shook my head.

"Not yet," I replied, unable to see her through the large windows at the front of the establishment. We waited in the car, trying to remain unseen in the spreading dusk of evening. At almost half past six,

Cara came around the corner and made her way along the street to the café. She headed inside, spoke briefly to a woman seated at a table before exiting the café. Glancing about her, she began to walk down the street as the woman she'd met with inside the building raced out to catch up with her. Johnny and I threw a quick glance at each other before jumping out of the car and following them as swiftly as we could without giving ourselves away. Cara never turned around, instead calling out for the other woman to keep up with her. The woman fell into step behind Cara and they made their way down an alley that led out into the woods beyond.

"Why would they go into the woods? Do you reckon that woman helped her with Marie?" Johnny whispered to me as we sped along the streets and followed the direction they had taken. I didn't know how to answer that so I didn't, putting my finger against my lips to indicate to him to be quiet. We saw the pair enter the woods, darkness shrouding them completely so we raced across the space between us and the woods, coming to a halt just past the first set of trees.

"Which way now?" I muttered, annoyed that I couldn't see where they had gone. We listened for a moment and then we heard it.

"Cara? What the hell is this? What are you doing?" a feminine voice shrieked in panic. Johnny and I didn't wait to hear any more. We ran in the direction the voice had come from, hoping we weren't going to be too late to help her.

"AAARGH!"

A bone chilling scream rang out across the area, followed by more frantic screams as we pushed harder to get to the woman. As we neared a small clearing in the woods, we could see Cara and what seemed like fifty odd other people. I came to an abrupt stop as Johnny crouched down behind a bush near the edge of the clearing. He tugged my hand so I joined him as we watched. We couldn't take on that many people but wait...was that a severed hand lying on the ground a few feet in front of us? I squinted in the twilight at the thing, gasping quietly when I saw that yes, it was a hand. I tried to get Johnny's attention to point it out but saw that he was transfixed in horror at the scene before us. I focused my attention back on the people who were with Cara, realising that the woman had stopped screaming. All I could hear was grunting noises and a little bit of squelching. Confused, I searched the faces of the people in the clearing, my mouth dropping open in terror at the sight.

These weren't people. Yes, they had been at some point but they weren't any longer. These were creatures that should have been buried and stayed that way. Torn clothes, emaciated figures, skin mottled and grey. Chunks of flesh missing from some whilst limbs were missing from others. All of them appeared to have no eyes, or at least, decaying eyes. How could they see what they were doing? The thing that made me want to gag the most was the source of the squelching. A person lay on the ground as these things *fed* on them. With a heavy heart, I realised it must be the woman we'd heard screaming. I shut my eyes, trying to force the image of her half eaten carcass out of my mind when I felt Johnny wrap his arm around my shoulders. I leaned into his side, grateful for the support. Was this what had happened to Marie? It made me want to be sick.

We stayed hidden behind our little cluster of bushes as Cara made her way over to the woman that was now dead. Holding a dark round object in her hands, she placed it on the body and began to chant. I felt Johnny's arm tighten as we watched, my own hands raised to my mouth at what we were witnessing. The air appeared to shimmer around us as the army of dead people stood still. A silvery light appeared to snake its way out of the body of the fallen woman, hovering over the round object as it emerged then slowly, it made its way upwards. It floated into Cara's open mouth, the silvery trail disappearing from sight until she closed her mouth and grinned. The small brunette opened her arms out wide in a grand gesture.

"Thankyou my lovely creatures. We've both gotten what we wanted out of this tonight! There are a few more witches in this village that I need to drain and then we'll be moving on!" Cara announced proudly. I furrowed my brows. More witches to drain? That could only mean she was going to kill again using these awful creatures! Even as I thought it, the zombies left the clearing, making their way further into the woods. Were they hiding in the woods until she called on them again? I shuddered at the thought. How many people would go camping there with that danger hidden amongst them? When it was only Cara left in the clearing, Johnny and I waited to see what she would do. Instead of leaving, she called out in a sing song voice:

"I know you're watching me! Come out and face me if you dare!"

I froze. I felt Johnny's arm trembling so I placed my hand on his knee, hoping it might calm him down from doing anything rash. The problem was that he wasn't afraid to face her, he would square up to her if it had just been him. Thankfully he took the hint and remained where he was, giving my shoulder a light squeeze in reassurance. As the minutes ticked by, I wondered if she was going to come looking for us. Laughter rang out in the silence as Cara turned in a full circle where she stood.

"Aww, don't you want to play? That's ok. You can tell people whatever you want, nobody will believe you! I will give you this one warning though, if you get in my way it will be the last thing you do. My friends will come for you and then, I'll turn you into one of them! See ya!" she called out.

With that, she ran away through the trees in a different direction to the one we'd come through. When the leaves stopped rustling and the air around us was quiet once more, I let out the breath I hadn't realised I was holding. Peeking up at Johnny's face, I saw that he had visibly relaxed too now that the crazy woman had gone.

"Johnny? How the hell do we stop *that*?"

Chapter Four.

We rode back to Johnny's house without saying a word to one another. It was too much to put into words. Cara was the killer, or at least she was in charge of the things that killed the two women. I couldn't wrap my head around it. Was Cara a witch? If so, who were the other witches she had spoken of? And what was the importance of their deaths? That silvery light had left the body of the woman who'd died and gone into Cara. Was she stealing their powers? I rubbed at my temples as a dull throbbing began to grow inside my head. When we arrived, Johnny invited me inside so I followed, trudging along behind him, not knowing what to say. The defeated stoop of his shoulders told me he didn't know how to proceed either.

He quietly made us both a drink and handed me a mug of coffee when it was ready, gesturing for me to follow him into his living room. It was a nice living space with cream walls and brown furniture that all matched. It was quite neat and tidy too, with everything having its own place. I sat down upon one of the armchairs whilst Johnny sat down upon the sofa, his face taut and pale. I took a sip of my coffee, ideas rushing through my mind of what we could do to help the unknown women but just as quickly, they disappeared as I realised they wouldn't work. I glanced back over at Johnny who was staring into space contemplatively. When I couldn't stand the silence anymore, I spoke up.

"So...what do you think we can do?"

He cocked his head slightly as he peered at me, the haunted expression back on his face. Poor Johnny, he was taking this hard.

"I'm not sure if I'm honest," came his low reply. "Is she even human?"

I shrugged my shoulders at that, cursing inwardly when I spilt some of the coffee over the rim of the cup onto my trouser leg. Rubbing at it as I tried to be inconspicuous, I pondered his question. Was she human? Or something else entirely?

"I don't know. She mentioned witches so I'm guessing that maybe she's a witch? I mean, that light that went from the other woman into Cara…do you reckon that was magic? Maybe she's stealing powers from other witches?" I asked, aware how crazy I sounded even as I said it. "I've no idea. It's the only thing that makes any kind of sense. Although if you'd asked me an hour ago if I believed in witches or zombies I would've said you were crazy! But now? I can't really deny what I've seen with my own eyes can I?"

Johnny shook his head, a wry smile playing upon his lips.

"At least you know it's not *just* you who's going crazy," he muttered. He rubbed at his eyes, sighing as he did so. "I don't know what our next move should be. You heard her, she's going to keep killing until she's got what she's wanted but if we interfere, she'll set those things on us too. How'd she even know we were there? I was sure she didn't see us!"

"I have no idea. Maybe it's part of her magic? I'm not sure what we can do either but that's more because we don't know anything about what we're dealing with. Perhaps we can try and find some information? That could be our next step. Know our enemy first, that kind of thing?"

Johnny leant forwards as he stared at me with a twinkle in his eye. His lips spread wide into a grin.

"That's a great idea! We can have a look and see if there's anyone that identifies as a witch in this village and go ask them! They can't all be bad right? I mean, if Marie was a witch then there must be more like her. She was so kind to everyone." Johnny slumped back into his seat as suddenly as he'd had the idea. "Who would we ask though? I didn't know anyone was a witch in this place and now there's a bunch of them!"

I thought about this for a few minutes. Who could we ask? He was right about the fact neither of us knew there were any witches until today but that didn't mean we couldn't get the information we needed. I racked my brain to think who might know the answers we needed. I drained the rest of my coffee as my mind ticked over, a flash of inspiration grabbing me out of the blue.

"I know who we can ask!" I exclaimed, annoyed I didn't think of it straight away. Johnny raised an eyebrow at me as I yanked my mobile phone from my trouser pocket and started searching for a number. He didn't speak or interrupt me when I dialled the number I wanted and waited for the other person to answer. It didn't take long to wait. Three rings and I heard the click on the other end to indicate they'd answered.

"Hey Anna. Is everything alright?" came the voice on the other end of the phone.

"It's great now I'm speaking with you," I announced happily. "You were close to Marie right? Any chance you knew what she was into and perhaps do it yourself?"

There was a long pause as I waited for the person to speak.

"What exactly are you after Anna?"

I mentally squealed in excitement. I was right! They would have the answers we needed, I knew it.

"Can Johnny and I come over tomorrow morning and see you? It's important and I think it might help to save you from ending up the same way as Marie. We know who did it," I told them, not wanting to give everything away until they'd agreed to see us.

"Alright. Come by at nine."

With another click, the line went dead. I turned to face Johnny who was watching me curiously. I smiled smugly at him, knowing he wanted to know who I'd spoken to.

"Who was that?" Johnny asked.

"Isla," I answered with the smile still in place.

"How'd you figure out that she was one?"

"She's one of Marie's best friends. It makes sense doesn't it? I don't know why I didn't think of her to start with to be honest.

We're meeting her at nine in the morning alright?" I informed him, knowing he wouldn't say no. He wanted answers as much as I did and we were in this together now, especially after what we'd witnessed with Cara. He nodded his agreement, lifting his arm to see the clock face of his watch.

"That's great but it's getting late. Did you need to get back home? If not, you're welcome to crash here and have a takeaway with me," he offered. I was a little taken aback. Johnny had never offered to hang out with me on my own before and I wasn't sure if it was a great idea. It was perfectly platonic on his side of course, but I didn't exactly want him to see me with bedhead in the morning.

"I don't have a toothbrush or anything with me," I muttered weakly. I knew it was a poor excuse but it was all the defense I had. Johnny chuckled.

"That's fine. I've got a spare one you can use and I don't mind lending you toiletries and something to wear if that's what you're worried about. Stay. Have a chill out night with me. I think we deserve it don't you?" he queried, a warm smile on his boyish face. How could I resist that? I smiled back at him.

"Sure, ok. What takeaway are you planning to persuade me with?" I laughed as I settled back into my armchair.

"Pizza? Can't go wrong with pizza can we?" he suggested, knowing I loved the stuff. I agreed. He placed the order and then turned back to me and asked what film I fancied watching with him. I raised an eyebrow at him.

"Film? I don't know what you've got so you can choose," I told him, happy to see the playful Johnny back for the time being. I studied him as he moved over to his cabinet by his television, perusing over his film choices before pulling out a dvd for us. He flashed the cover at me then placed it in the player. I chuckled at his choice. A romcom? Definitely not the genre of film I thought he'd choose, or even own. He'd always seemed more like the action type. It's funny how you can know someone for years without truly knowing them. He settled back down on his sofa and pressed play on the remote control. After a moment, he turned his head at me inquiringly.

"Are you going to come and sit next to me or keep sitting over there like a loner?" he asked. I didn't know how to react to that. He wanted me to sit next to him? I stood up slowly, making my way over to the sofa he was sat upon and slid down onto the seat next to him. He held his arm out just above my shoulders for me to slide up next to him. I did so hesitantly, nervous when he draped his arm around me when I leant against the side of his body. What was going on here? This was very intimate for us. Other than the occasional hug or pulling each other along by the hands, we'd never cuddled before. This was completely new territory for me, and my heart was pounding. Should I say something? Do something? I was tense, unsure what to do with myself.

"Would you relax?" he whispered into my ear, his breath warm against my skin. I swallowed hard, trying to force myself to calm down. I decided to try and ignore that

I was cuddled up with my secret crush and concentrate on the movie instead. It was the best idea as I was soon laughing at the tomfoolery that I witnessed on the screen. I felt Johnny's body trembling from the laughter that racked his own body, his warmth seeping into every part of me that was touching him.

Ding dong!

The doorbell rang loudly, causing us to both jump at the sound. We chuckled at our reactions, realising it was the events of the evening that had made us both so wary. Johnny leapt up from his spot to go and answer the door to fetch the pizza. I heard him chatting to the delivery driver for a few minutes before he came back to me with the boxes in his hands.

"Want any plates?" he asked.

"No I'm good. The box is fine," I replied. He grinned at me, sitting back down next to me with the boxes on his lap. Looking at the one he picked up first, he handed it to me and then opened his own box. I breathed in deeply. It smelled delicious. I'd gone for a bbq chicken pizza whereas he'd gone for a meat feast. We sat and munched on our food as we carried on watching the film in companionable silence. I was glad I agreed to spend tonight at his house, chilling out with him. After the events of the past few days, this was nice and a bit of normality we both needed. If I didn't include the cuddling and the staying over and the fact that it was just the two of us, I could pretend it was one of our nights hanging out with friends. This was different of course, but it still held enough familiarity for it to be pleasant. The film finished at about the same time as we ate the last of our pizzas, so Johnny suggested we put another one on. Considering we needed to let our food go down a bit before going to bed, I agreed. This time, he chose an action film. There it was, the type of film I'd imagined Johnny being into. I chuckled to myself as he started it up, causing him to turn to me and ask what was funny.

"Nothing," I replied, unable to help another chuckle. At the imploring look on his face, I gave in and let him in on the joke. "Well, when you pulled out the first film, I was really surprised you were into those types of films as I'd always figured you to be an action type of guy. Now, you've chosen an action film and I just couldn't help but find it funny."

I saw the amusement on his face as he accepted my words and leaned backwards, pulling me back into his side. I nestled against him more comfortably this time, the shock of earlier having worn off. I enjoyed being like this with him. It made me feel safe and secure, even if it was only for a short time. The film was full of action, keeping me gripped. At one point it startled me and my hand landed on Johnny's leg by accident. Before I could move it away though, he placed his free hand over mine and held it in place, intertwining his fingers with mine. That was it, my heart began pounding again. What was going on here? Was he into me after all? I kept my mouth shut, not wanting to ask and ruin the whole thing in case I was reading the situation wrong. After all, he could just be being friendly and holding my hand as a comfort for the more surprising scenes in the film. I squeezed my eyes shut, counted to ten to focus on calming myself down, then went back to concentrating on the film. I needed to pull myself together.

"So what did you think?" Johnny asked as the film ended.

"Yeah, it was good actually. Is there another one to explain what happens to the guys at the end? Left it a bit open there didn't they?" I replied, attempting to move away from him to sit up properly. He didn't move or let go of me, holding me in place. I turned my head to face him, puzzled. "Johnny? Is everything alright?"

He smiled softly at me, gazing at me tenderly as he did so. He nodded his head slightly, leaning closer to me as his eyes swept down to my lips. Before I could register what he was doing, he closed the distance between us and pressed his lips against mine, his hands coming up to cup my face between them. When he pulled his face away to gaze at me, I remained where I was in utter shock. Did that really just happen? Johnny frowned, pursing his lips as he searched my eyes for whatever it was he was looking for.

"I'm sorry," he said as he let his hands fall from my face. "I shouldn't have done that."

"No it's ok!" I told him quickly, realising my reaction hadn't been very encouraging at all. I placed my hand on his arm, preventing him from moving any further away from me. He hesitated, watching me cautiously. "It was a very nice kiss…I just wasn't expecting it. I froze, I'm sorry."

"Was it unwelcome then?" he enquired warily. I smiled softly at him then, my eyes softening as I gazed fondly at him.

"Not unwelcome at all. In fact, I think you should try it again," I offered, aware I was blushing by the heat rising in my cheeks. Johnny's lips curled up in the corners as he slowly leaned towards me once again. This time, I met him halfway as our lips pressed together tenderly. Johnny applied a little more pressure as he swept his tongue along the seam of my lips and prompted them to part. I allowed him in, jostling my tongue against his as the moment overtook me with joy. This was the kiss I had been longing for for years and it didn't disappoint. After several minutes, we broke apart a little out of breath.

"Woah," Johnny breathed out. They were my sentiments too. "Do you want to sleep in my room tonight?" At the alarm on my face at his words, he quickly hastened to add; "not to do anything! I mean, to cuddle and you know, maybe kiss some more?"

"That'd be nice," I murmured shyly, unsure how this had come about. "I didn't even realise you liked me."

Johnny's eyes widened in surprise.

"You didn't? I've not exactly been subtle over the past few months. Truth be told, I wasn't sure you liked me, but the others all told me you did and when you didn't pull your hand away when I held yours during the film, I got my hopes up that perhaps I was wrong."

I stared at him for a moment before bursting out laughing. He seemed bemused, uncertain about what was funny so I tried to calm myself down so I could tell him.

"I'm sorry, I shouldn't laugh but it's too funny. There's you been thinking I didn't like you that way and I've been thinking the same thing! I guess we got our wires pretty crossed huh?" I managed to get out eventually. He snorted his amusement as he pondered this, coming to the same conclusion as me. How had I gotten him so wrong? He'd always behaved like a close friend and nothing more but I'd obviously been misreading the signals he'd sent me. Perhaps he'd been worried about ruining the friendship the same as I had and tried to hide his feelings? I chuckled again at myself, happy that we'd found out the truth before it was too late. Johnny took my hands in his, rubbing his thumbs across the backs of them as he gazed at me with a soft smile on his lips.

"How's about tomorrow night we go out for a proper date so there's no more confusion?" he asked me gently, a mischievous twinkle in his eye. I nodded my head back at him.

"Yeah, I'd love that. Come on, let's go get some sleep. We've still got to go and see Isla in the morning," I reminded him. Even with the dangerous threat hanging over us and our friends, I was jumping for joy at this turn of events. Perhaps this adventure of ours would lead to much better things in the end.

Chapter Five.

Getting up on that Saturday morning was hard.

Johnny's arms were wrapped tightly around me as he slept, his breath warming the back of my neck. I sighed in contentment as it all rushed back to me on waking up, the kisses, the confessions of liking each other. The date. The meeting with Isla. I frowned a little, remembering that the most important thing was finding out more about witches and how we could stop Cara. Romance was great but we needed to make our village safe from her first. I nudged at Johnny, telling him to wake up. As he groaned in response to my nudges, I rolled out of the bed and raced into the bathroom. Johnny had shown me where everything was the night before so I got myself ready, pulling on my clothes from the day before and went downstairs to make some coffee for us both. Johnny joined me after about ten minutes, his coffee cooling on the table as I drank mine. We didn't say much to each other, nervousness about what we were going to find out hanging in the air. Drinks finished, we headed out to my car and got in, ready to make our way over to Isla's.

"You ready for this?" Johnny muttered. I saw him watching me out of the corner of my eye as I pulled away from the house and drove to the other side of the village where Isla lived. It wouldn't take us long to get there.

"Yes. At least, I think so. I don't know what we're going to find but I'm hoping we can help in some way," I replied, deciding to be honest with him. Who knew what we were going to find out? I hoped that Isla really did know about witches and would give us the information we needed to protect the remaining witches from Cara, otherwise I wasn't sure where else to look. We pulled up outside her house a few minutes later, taking in the beautiful sand-coloured stones it was made of with a slanted tile roof. The front garden was immaculate with various flowers dotted about in stylish clusters. I remembered how I'd always wondered how she found the time to make her garden and house look so amazing when she was busy with her job and extra hours put in to fundraising for charities. Now it made more sense. She was probably using magic to help her with it all. I knew it might not be but it just seemed the most logical reasoning. I knew she didn't use a gardener to help her or a cleaner, she'd always prided herself on having a pristine house and garden done by herself.

We got out of the car and made our way up to the front of the house, pressing the doorbell when we came to a halt.

"Come in!" a voice called out from inside. I pushed the door open, immediately feeling my worries slip away when I stepped inside as though someone had just washed them all away. I blinked in surprise, moving out of Johnny's way when I saw that he had the same expression on his face.

"Wow, that's amazing! I feel so much lighter than I did five minutes ago. Do you?" I asked Johnny, shocked that I didn't feel any sadness or fear anymore. Johnny nodded his head in agreement. Slowly, we made our way forwards until we came to a large living room where we could see Isla seated in an armchair near a large window. The light from the window seemed to bathe her in a warm glow, making her appear almost angelic to our eyes. I stepped into the room first with Johnny on my heels.

Isla appeared older than usual, her hair beginning to grey and wrinkles were appearing on her forehead. I knew she was older than Marie and the rest of us but at this moment, she looked it. She gazed sadly at us when she raised her eyes to us but she gave a small smile and pointed to the sofa for us to have a seat. We sat ourselves down on the leather sofa, waiting to see if she would speak. Isla regarded us both for a minute, peering over her glasses at us.

"So," she began. "You wanted to speak with me."

I cleared my throat and straightened my shoulders as I did so, preparing to tell her what we knew.

"Yes, that's right. I'm not sure how else to say this so I'm just going to come out and say it. We know Marie was a witch and we know how she died. As you were her best friend, we figured there was a possibility that you might be one too and if you are, that you might be able to help us to stop the person who is behind the deaths," I blurted out quickly.

The other woman's eyebrows raised at this, confusion flitting across her features.

"Sorry but did you say deaths? As in plural?" she asked.

"Yes. Marie and another lady who we don't know," came the deep voice of Johnny by my side. I felt his hand creep along my arm and come to a rest on top of my own hand, snaking his fingers between mine in reassurance. I smiled gratefully at him. He seemed to ground me as I continued our conversation.

"There's a witch, or at least it looks very much like a witch, that is doing this and it's going to sound incredibly silly but she's using zombies or undead or whatever you want to call them to kill people who are witches. We came to you because we hoped you could give us some more information so we can try to stop her and obviously, to warn you about her as well," I informed her, noting the alarm on her face.

Isla leaned forward in her chair conspiratorially, a sliver of grey hair falling across her eyes. She swept it out of her way absentmindedly.

"That sounds very grave indeed. I think you're going to need to tell me the whole story and I shall believe what you say because you were right to assume I practice just like Marie did. I'm glad that you have come to me, so please tell me. Tell me the whole thing," she encouraged.

So we did. Johnny told her about the night with Marie first, about the phone call and when he arrived to see Cara walking from the scene. Then I told her about my visit to Cara's house then the trip to the café where she met the other woman she had killed and the events that happened afterwards in the woods. By the time we finished telling the story, I felt drained. The good feeling from when we'd walked in had vanished, leaving behind the same empty, scared feeling I'd felt since we'd seen the zombies. Isla sat back in her chair silent, thinking upon what we had just told her, her face slack. After a couple of minutes, she seemed to pull herself together. She blinked and turned her gaze upon us once again.

"So Cara is killing witches? I didn't even realise she was one! We usually give off an aura so that other witches can identify us but I haven't got that from Cara," she muttered, more to herself than me and Johnny.

"So you don't think she's a witch?" Johnny ventured, leaning forwards in his own seat now. His hand remained clasped around mine.

"No, no. She's almost certainly a witch but it would seem she's very powerful if she can hide her aura from the rest of us. Can you just explain what happened when Cara was chanting again? I just want to be clear on this," Isla asked, staring me directly in the eyes. I gulped at the intensity of her gaze and nodded my head.

"Of course. The woman was dead on the ground at that point from what I could see and Cara pulled out this round object and put it on the woman's body-" Isla cut me off.

"What did the object look like?" she queried.

"I don't know," I replied, feeling a bit lost. "We were too far away to really see and it was dark. All I could make out was that it was a roundish shape."

Isla pursed her lips but bade me to carry on with what I was telling her.

"When she placed the object on the woman, Cara began to chant something but again, I couldn't make out the words. This silvery light appeared as if it was escaping from the woman's body on the ground and then it went up into Cara's mouth. It was such a bright light, that's how I was able to see it. It might sound daft but I thought it might possibly be the woman's powers and Cara was stealing them but of course, I have absolutely no idea and that's just speculation. What do you think it could be?" I put the question to Isla but she was already smiling at me, her eyes twinkling.

"You're right. That light would have been her powers and it seems that Cara is stealing powers from other witches. It would explain why she is killing them, although what she would want with all that power, I dare not imagine." Isla was quiet for a moment, "I think I need to call a meeting of the witches in this village and warn them all about Cara. You certainly did the right thing in bringing this matter to me and I can't thank you enough."

"What do we do now?" Johnny asked before I could ask the same question. Isla shook her head and waved her hands in front of her.

"No, you must do nothing. You're not equipped to deal with this situation. If Cara discovers you've helped us then it might put you both in danger," she told us fervently. I glanced down at my hands with a small frown, annoyed she was going to push us out of this now. Johnny had other ideas though.

"It's too late for that. Cara knows we were there. She gave us a warning already. She will know that we have told you so we've already got a target on our backs and we want to know how we can help you to stop her. I *need* to stop her," Johnny insisted, glaring at the older woman sat before us. I placed my hand on Johnny's arm in an effort to remind him to calm down. Isla hesitated, then inclined her head.

"Alright, as you wish. If anything happens then at least you'll know what you're walking into. Let me call the others up first and get them to come here as soon as they can and then I'll explain a bit more of our magic to you whilst we're waiting. When they're here, we can come up with some sort of plan. OK?" she asked. Not waiting for an answer, Isla stood up and made her way over to where her house phone and phonebook was to start making the calls. Five minutes later, she sat back down with us with a heavy sigh. I'd counted as she'd made the calls, counting six different people. I couldn't believe how many witches were in our village and I needed to ask her about it.

"How are there so many witches in this village and how do none of us know about it?"

Isla chuckled at my question, obviously amused.

"That would be because people only see what they want to see. The signs are all there but if you don't believe then you don't see. As for why we're here, well that's because this village is so peaceful and quiet and we can practise our craft without bothering anyone. Witches tend to like to stick together so we can protect each other if the need ever arises like this situation we find ourselves in. Now, let's run through some things you might like to know before the others get here shall we?"

It took almost two hours for everyone to arrive due to family or work commitments so whilst we waited, Isla explained the basics to us. For example, the rules that the witches follow to ensure they stay under the radar from the 'normal' people and when they tried to meet up such as on a full or new moon or for specific celebrations. Isla informed us that every witch had her own book where she wrote her spells down into for safe keeping and that the magic that Cara had been using was dark magic. Apparently, only extremely strong witches could conjure up the dead to do their bidding but if Cara had been collecting powers from witches from before she came to our village, then she was more powerful than anyone knew. I was shocked by the information I was given and found myself holding onto my cross-shaped necklace for comfort. I'd never really been a religious person but I liked the necklaces as they symbolised hope and at this point in time, I needed some hope.

When the six witches finally arrived at Isla's house, I gasped when I saw who they were. I knew all of these women and I had never suspected a thing! Johnny squeezed my hand to remind me he was with me so I found myself calming down a little. I was being silly; these women were no more a threat to me than Johnny was. I knew them and they were all good, kind-hearted ladies. They appeared confused and wary when they saw Jonny and myself sitting on Isla's sofa but she told them it was fine before launching straight into the whole sorry tale.

I watched the emotions that crossed their faces: anger, disgust, horror, surprise and finally, gratefulness when they heard that Johnny and I had brought this to them to warn them all. Murmured thanks went around the room before the discussion of how they were going to stop Cara started. My ears pricked up at this. I wanted to know what they planned to do as did Johnny. We leaned forwards nonchalantly so as not to bring attention to ourselves as they argued over what they would do. It felt as though hours were passing by as they threw various ideas back and forth and I found myself getting very frustrated. My stomach rumbled, alerting me to the fact we hadn't eaten in a long time and were still no further forward. I coughed slightly to get their attention. The witches stopped talking, all of them turning to face me as one. I gulped. I hated when people stared at me like this.

"I'm sorry to interrupt but we're not getting anywhere. I've heard some good ideas and bad ones over the time you've all been discussing this but you seem to have forgotten the main focus of it. We need to stop Cara. You're all discussing what to do with her once you've caught and stopped her but where's the ideas to actually stop her? I don't mean any offense but I had to ask," I told them, hoping they weren't about to turn me into a toad or similar. A few glared at me but Isla chuckled.

"You're right, you're absolutely right. We haven't figured out the solution to the main problem yet. Do *you* have any suggestions Anna?" she asked, quirking an eyebrow as she waited for my response.

"Umm, well you could maybe lure her into a trap. Like, I could ask her to meet me somewhere and you could all be nearby to cast a spell on her when she's there? I'm not really sure what you can do so I'm not the best to ask but it's an idea. I don't mind being bait if that helps," I told them, grimacing when I heard the strangled sound coming from Johnny's direction.

"What are you doing?" he demanded, putting his mouth close to my ear so I was the only one who could hear him. "You could get hurt!"

"I know but two people are already dead and we need to stop Cara. If we don't, she's going to kill all of these women here and we've grown up with these people! We can't risk them dying just because we're scared we might get hurt," I whispered back loudly. I lifted my head as I faced Isla. "I want to do it. I want to help."

I felt Johnny let go of my arm and sink back into his chair, his mouth turned down at the corners as he sulked. He wasn't happy but he'd have to get over it. Isla walked over to me and clasped my hand in her own.

"Are you sure about this Anna? If you do want to help then we would be glad of it. It's a very good plan of yours actually so we just need to figure out what we will do once you get her in one spot for us," Isla said, smiling down at me. I nodded my agreement before she let go and went back to discussing their plan now that they had something to work with. I could see Johnny was still in a mood with me for the remainder of the time we were there but I didn't mind. I knew I was doing the right thing and deep down, so did he. Once the plan was finalised, I used the phonebook to find Cara's number and called her up. The phone rang a couple of times before she answered.

"Hello?" came her falsely sweet voice.

"Cara, it's Anna. I need to talk with you. Can you meet me at the back of Newman's? I'm meeting Johnny there for a drink but I need to chat with you first," I lied to her, hoping it was believable enough for her to agree.

"Fine. What time?"

My heart leapt into my throat so I tried to keep my voice calm as I told her to meet me there in an hour before hanging up the phone. I faced the others who were watching me with smiles on their faces and Isla beamed at me.

"Good girl. Right ladies and gent," Isla called out, winking over at Johnny as he came to join us all. "Let's get to business shall we? Let's rid our home of this evil creature and make it safe once more!"

The others cheered so Johnny and I joined in, a feeling of elation filling me up as I realised that we were going to stop Cara in her tracks. She wasn't going to be able to hurt anyone ever again after tonight!

Chapter Six.

An hour later and everyone was in their places.

I stood by the side of my car, leaning against it as I waited for Cara to arrive. Johnny was sitting in Newman's, keeping an eye on me through the window so that if Cara saw him inside she'd know that I really was meeting him for a drink like I told her. Isla and the witches were hiding at various points around the carpark, hidden from sight so that Cara wouldn't see them until it was too late. The plan had hatched that Cara would be trapped to the area by my car with a two metre radius all around so that she wouldn't realise straightaway she was trapped. Then, once that was done the witches would use the same spell on Cara as she had done on the dead witch to take her powers away from her. Yes, it would make them stronger but it would eliminate Cara as a threat and they would be able to dispose of her in a way that was fitting for a traitorous witch. Neither Johnny nor myself had asked what that meant, we knew we probably wouldn't like it so we chose to ignore it if it meant that Cara wouldn't be able to hurt anyone ever again. I glanced towards Johnny, giving him a small wave and smile to alleviate his concerns as best as I could. He gave me a tight smile in return but his eyes went wide as Cara passed by the window in front of him. I squared my shoulders as she made her way over to me, planting my feet firmly on the ground and took a step away from my vehicle. The slight woman stopped in front of me, a bemused expression on her face.

"Hey Anna," she said brightly. "To what do I owe this pleasure?"

I smiled, happy in the knowledge she was falling for our plan. Even now, I knew the witches would be chanting their spell to keep her here.

"I wanted to chat with you about what you're doing. You need to stop."

Cara laughed out loud at my words, her dark hair bouncing as her body vibrated with the emotion.

"And you think you can stop me? That's hilarious!" she cried, still chuckling at me. I shook my head.

"No, not me. The other witches though? Yeah, I reckon they stand a chance at stopping you."

She stopped laughing then, her whole body going rigid as the realisation hit her that I'd gone to others about her. She took a step closer to me.

"What have you done?" she hissed at me, her eyes flashing with anger. I inadvertently took a step backwards from her, attempting to put a bit more space between us. I suddenly realised the huge flaw with this plan. Cara was stuck in this space by my car but would I be able to get out unharmed? I felt the blood drain from my face as this knowledge hit me. Damn! Why didn't I realise this sooner? I hoped the witches would protect me from the crazy woman in front of me.

"I warned them about you," I informed her, deciding to be brave in the hopes it might help me get through the next few minutes. "They know you're stealing powers and that you're coming for them."

"You stupid cow!" Cara roared, closing the space between us and slapped me across the face. I fell against the side of my car from the force of it, tremulously grabbing the place where she'd hit me. I could feel the heat of it against my hand.

"You leave her alone!" I heard Johnny's voice before I saw him, already running towards us both. Cara rolled her eyes as she faced him, heading in his direction. Johnny stopped running, realising that she was about to find out that she was trapped. I saw the pleading on his face to get out of there so I ran to the side, away from the invisible circle we'd trapped her in even as I saw the witches coming out of their hiding places. Cara kept walking forwards until she bumped into an invisible barrier.

"Oof!" The sound sprang from her mouth involuntarily and the witches immediately surrounded her in her circle. Cara eyed them all warily, turning about slowly as she took them all in. A wide grin spread slowly across her face as she took it all in.

"Oh, you've all come to see me? How kind of you to make it all so much easier for me," she spat out, the grin still in place. Grunting noises could be heard in the approaching darkness behind us so I turned around to see what the noise was. Oh no! I saw a small army of the dead creatures lumbering towards us, coming from all sides to close us off from one another. I heard Isla shout instructions to the other witches as they all turned their backs on Cara to deal with the zombies she'd set upon us all. I glanced over to Johnny and ran over to him, wanting to be by his side if anything happened. Johnny grabbed my arm as I reached him, pulling me in tight against his side as we watched the horror unfurling before us. The zombies had already reached the witches, all of them surrounded by at least a dozen each. We heard the screams from the witches, unable to see what was happening. I held on tightly to Johnny, fear coursing through me. Were they alright? Why weren't the zombies coming for us? I took a peek at Cara as the madness ensued. She was simply stood, staring out at the carpark around us as her zombies attacked the witches. She was still smiling. I frowned at that. What was she happy about? The witches would defeat her zombies then make her pay. Wouldn't they? The zombies continued their attack, the screams from the witches dying down until there was only silence. Cara clapped her hands loudly, causing the zombies to stop what they were doing. They began to shuffle off from the carpark, heading into the woods as the bodies of the witches were revealed. Torn pieces of limbs lay strewn about the ground in bloody chunks. I screamed as Johnny held onto me. I could feel his heart thudding beneath my hands as I saw Cara stalk over to us. I felt the panic rising within me as I realised we had lost.

"Johnny? What do we do?" I whispered frantically, moving backwards until he wrapped his arms around me and enveloped my body against his. I felt the slight tremble in his hands as he shrugged. There wasn't much he could say. We both knew what Cara was capable of and our only hope of defeating her had been the witches. Cara came to a halt in front of us.

"Well, your plan didn't exactly work out did it? They're all dead now and so is the trapping spell. Oh don't worry, I'm not going to kill either of you," she told us as we waited to meet our fates. My eyes widened in surprise at her words.

"You're…you're not?" I stuttered, unable to believe my ears. She'd promised we would pay if we tried to stop her so what was happening here?

"Of course not! Why would I do that when I can make you pay in other ways?" she asked innocently. Before we had a chance to move or try to escape, Cara was upon us. She threw me out of the way as she reached out for Johnny and grabbed him by the throat. He struggled but she chanted under her breath, causing him to freeze. She grabbed his chin, forcing him to look her directly in the eyes.

"You will leave this place. You will forget about Anna and your friends here and think of this place only as a place you had to leave. You won't ever look back or want to return. You'll go now. Pack your bags and leave."

Johnny's eyes had misted over as she spoke but they cleared after a moment, nodding his head slowly as he acknowledged what she'd said. Without a second glance at me, he began to walk away.

"No! Johnny!" I cried out, taking a step to go after him but Cara blocked my path. Her eyes narrowed at me as I peeked over her shoulder to watch Johnny disappearing from my life. When he was gone, I put my full attention on her. "What did you do?"

"I made him forget about you and everything here that matters to him. He'll be alright, he'll go and live somewhere else and not think about any of this again," Cara informed me with a sly smile. "You on the other hand, you won't get such an easy fate. I warned you not to interfere didn't I? Yet you chose to go to the witches and tell them, not that it did anyone any good. They're dead and I'll take their powers from them once I'm done with you."

Fear took over me at her words. I was angry about Johnny but self-preservation was beginning to kick in.

"What are you going to do?" I asked, backing away from her whilst searching for some kind of escape route. She reached out and grabbed my arm, halting me from moving. She shook me hard.

"You're not going anywhere. I think I'll take you with me so that you can see everything I do from now on and know just how badly you failed," she said sinisterly.

With that, I felt a burning sensation cover my whole body as everything seemed to grow larger around me. Was I shrinking? A red film covered my vision as I shrank, getting smaller and smaller as something hard pressed against the length of my back. I tried to turn but found I couldn't. I screamed as the panic overtook me, wondering what was going on until the red film enveloping my vision became hard and

I realised it was encasing me completely. I gazed up at Cara from where I lay on the ground, encased in this red rock. She seemed to be a giant! Bending down, she picked me up from off the ground, smiling at my predicament.

"Aww, look! Now you're just a pretty necklace! You'll be able to see everything I do but you won't be able to do a single thing to stop me. Perfect isn't it?" she muttered, taking the chain of the necklace I was now entombed in and placing it over her head. I found myself facing outwards from her body, moving as she made her way over to the bodies of the witches. They were in pieces, the parts of their bodies strewn about the ground. I gagged but couldn't move to even cover my mouth. Oh, this was awful! I watched on in silent fury as Cara used the round object to steal the powers from the fallen witches, laughing to herself as she did. She knew I could hear her. Upon closer inspection, I saw the round object was actually a small skull, perhaps belonging to an animal? I couldn't tell.

As Cara finished up, I surveyed the horror she had wrought upon our village. So many people were dead thanks to her. I felt the tears welling up in my eyes, falling down as the injustice of it all washed over me. How could she get away with this? It wasn't fair! I watched the direction we began to head in, wondering where she was taking us. As if she had heard my thoughts, I heard her speak.

"Oh don't worry Anna. I'm finished here so we're going to go on a trip of our own. I've got some people to see."

The End.

If you want to find out what happens next, this story will be continued in Madame Midnight...

Printed in Great Britain
by Amazon